D1579311

THE DISGUSTING ADVENTURES OF

FLEABAG MONKEYFACE

MOLDFINGER

KNIFE & PACKER

WALKER
BOOKS

The authors would like to dedicate this book to the
inventor of the garden composter, without whom we
would all be piling up compost at home!

First published 2010 by Walker Books Ltd
87 Vauxhall Walk, London SE11 5HJ

2 4 6 8 10 9 7 5 3

© 2010 Duncan McCoshan and Jem Packer

The right of Duncan McCoshan and Jem Packer to be identified
as author/illustrator of this work has been asserted by them
in accordance with the Copyright, Designs and Patents Act 1988

This book has been typeset in Shinn Light

Printed and bound in Great Britain by Clays Ltd, St Ives plc

British Library Cataloguing in Publication Data:
a catalogue record for this book is available
from the British Library

ISBN 978-1-4063-2433-4

www.walker.co.uk

A NOTE FROM THE PUBLISHER

We apologize for what you are about to read!

You may find the images of **genetically modified monstrous mushrooms** disturbing...

We suggest that while reading you steer clear of **mushroom pizzas**, avoid **mushroom soup** at all costs – crossing the street, if necessary – and body-swerve any **mushroom omelettes**.

Because this story contains scenes of **extreme mouldiness**.

So don't tell us we didn't warn you!

But before we get to the horrible mouldy stuff, let's meet our heroes, **Gerald**, **Gene** and **Fleabag Monkeyface**. Here's a few things you need to know about them:

Gene
Likes: Making lists, especially of gross things
Dislikes: Bunny rabbits
Favourite word: "Unreal"
You should know: Gene has the ideas

Gerald
Likes: The sound of a toilet flushing
Dislikes: Clean towels
Favourite word: "Cool"
You should know: Gerald has the stupid habit of liking Gene's ideas

Fleabag Monkeyface
Likes: Eating nits
Dislikes: Baths, showers and soap
Favourite word: "Ug-brilliant"
You should know: He's got Gross-Out Power

Without Gerald, Gene and Fleabag, the world would be a much cleaner, shinier place. But let's start at the beginning...

1 Gerald, Gene and Fleabag Monkeyface could hardly contain their excitement – they had front-row seats for the latest **Brock Moleman: Secret Agent film**. Gerald and Gene were tucking into popcorn and hotdogs from the cinema shop, but Fleabag had brought his own snacks with him.

"My home-grown ug-mushrooms," he said, opening a box to reveal the stinking fungi. "And all covered in my ug-own recipe salsa. Ug-delicious!"

"Cool!" said Gerald.

"Unreal!" said Gene.

Now, unlike most people, Gerald, Gene and Fleabag LOVED gross home-grown produce...

In fact, Gerald, Gene and Fleabag's love of gross-out was always getting them into trouble and this wasn't the first time they'd grown something unpleasant.

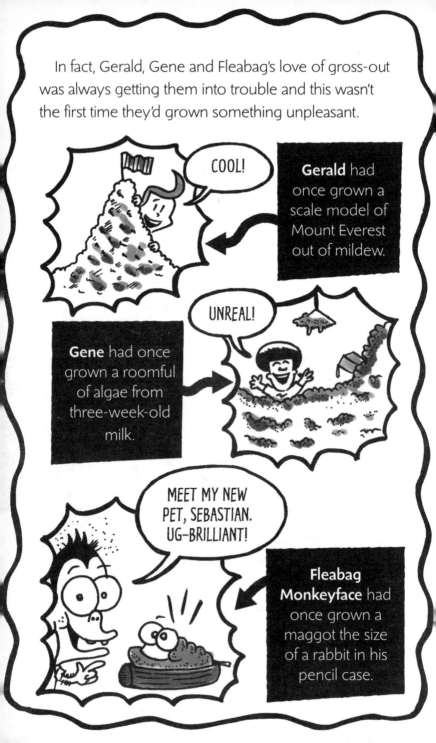

COOL!

Gerald had once grown a scale model of Mount Everest out of mildew.

UNREAL!

Gene had once grown a roomful of algae from three-week-old milk.

MEET MY NEW PET, SEBASTIAN. UG-BRILLIANT!

Fleabag Monkeyface had once grown a maggot the size of a rabbit in his pencil case.

Back at the cinema, Gerald, Gene and Fleabag were loving the film. **Brock Moleman** was based on a real-life legendary secret service agent – a suave special agent who protected the world from gross-out disasters. He was their favourite action hero!

In *The Man with the Golden Dung*, Brock Moleman was back doing what he did best...

YOU'LL NEVER DESTROY THE EARTH WITH YOUR DEADLY DUNG-GUN, SCARAMANGEY...

Using a host of gadgets and taking on any terrain – no matter how gross!

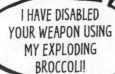

I HAVE DISABLED YOUR WEAPON USING MY EXPLODING BROCCOLI!

And saving the world from Gross-Out disaster.

YOUR MANURE MANSION IS FLATTENED. TIME FOR A CHILLED BEVERAGE TO CELEBRATE. ADIOS, SCARAMANGEY!!

On the way home, Gerald and Gene talked non-stop about the film – but Fleabag was very quiet.

He was in a rush to get back to the **Gross-Out Den**, where he was growing mushrooms for School Healthy Eating Week. The next day was the Grand Finale, and the whole school were bringing in their vegetables to try and create the biggest salad in the world – ever!

Fleabag had created a unique blend of **mega-super-strong compost**, and it was having a startling effect on his mushrooms. Not only were they the slimiest and mouldiest ever – they were also growing at an alarming rate!

Now, if you think using your own bedroom as a fungus farm is bad, then the ingredients in the compost are going to keep you awake at night!

GERALD, GENE AND FLEABAG MONKEYFACE'S RECIPE FOR PERFECT MEGA-SUPER-STRONG COMPOST

1 Take twenty-eight chicken bones, fourteen fish-heads and three hundred rinds of bacon.

2 Add rotting cabbage, sprouts and potato peel. Soak in two-year-old broccoli juice.

3 Place in a rusty bucket and leave for three weeks. Then remove and put in plant pots.

WEAR PROTECTIVE CLOTHING!!!

2 The next day Gerald, Gene and Fleabag took their **Gross-Out Mushrooms** to school. They also had their film gear with them.

When they weren't growing gross vegetables or watching Brock Moleman films, Gerald, Gene and Fleabag made films for their very own TV show – Gross-Out TV. The trouble was their adventures always seemed to get in the way of filming...

"I can't wait to capture the world-record attempt on film," said Gene excitedly.

"Let's hope something really gross happens when we add Fleabag's mushrooms!" Gerald chuckled as they walked through the school gates.

A colossal salad bowl filled the playground. Next to it, all the pupils were standing in a line, proudly holding their home-grown vegetables.

"We need to get into a good position to film this," said Gerald.

"How about up there?" suggested Gene, pointing at a large metal structure teetering above the bowl.

On the platform, they found their teacher, Mr Troutman. "I'd forgotten you'd been given permission to film," he muttered. "No funny business this time."

"You won't even know we're here," said Gerald.

Mr Troutman rolled his eyes before turning to address the school.

One by one, the children climbed up to the platform and handed their vegetables to Mr Troutman, who tossed them into the huge bowl.

But even with all the children's vegetables, the salad bowl was still nowhere near full.

"We have made a *big* salad, but not a *record-breaking* one," said Mr Troutman. "Fortunately, **Moldfinger Mushroom Technologies**, the world's largest mushroom manufacturer, has kindly agreed to top up our salad with a gigantic delivery of their own!"

"Hang on!" shouted Gerald. "We've grown a contribution too!"

"What have you brought? Beautiful beans? Radiant radishes? Gorgeous greens?" said Mr Troutman.

"No – **mushrooms**!" said Fleabag, holding out a bulging box.

3 Mr Troutman took the box, but before he could lift the lid, it burst open and the mushrooms exploded out, knocking him backwards. He landed bottom first in the salad bowl ... just as the lorry began unloading its mushrooms.

SPLAT!

All the children screeched. Mr Troutman was being buried alive!

"Mr Troutman!" cried Gerald, who in trying to grab him had only succeeded in dropping his camera into the bowl.

"I always knew too many vegetables were bad for you," said Gene, watching Mr Troutman disappear under a sea of salad.

"We need to do something!" cried Gerald. "Time for some **Gross-Out Power**, Fleabag!"

"Brock Moleman might not be here, but I ug-am! Ug-bionic banana breath!" said Fleabag, delivering a huge blast of putrid breath into the bowl.

At first nothing happened, but then the vegetables slowly started to froth and melt ... and their class teacher bobbed to the surface.

"Mr Troutman – you're alive!" said Gerald gleefully, and everyone cheered.

But Mr Troutman looked decidedly grumpy. "What is this ... this *stuff*?" he said. His face was green and not unlike the colour of rotten cabbage.

"Ug-mouldy soup!" said Fleabag. "My ug-breath liquidized the vegetables on contact. I ug-saved you!"

"Well, I wouldn't have needed 'ug-saving' in the first place if it hadn't been for your mushrooms," barked the angry teacher.

Mr Troutman had to do some serious grovelling before the Moldfinger driver agreed to take the putrid soup away.

As the lorry pulled off, Mr Troutman turned on Gerald, Gene and Fleabag. "I have no idea what that monstrous vegetable matter you brought in was, but I was almost crushed to death! As punishment, I want you to grow the tastiest salad **EVER** by the end of the month. And no weird mushy stuff!"

4 Gerald, Gene and Fleabag spent the next few weeks trying to make normal vegetables. They cut Fleabag's Gross-Out Mushrooms back, planted new seeds and covered them in compost. But the mushrooms kept on growing. In fact, they had soon outgrown the **Gross-Out Den** and were spreading outside.

"These mushrooms are getting out of hand," said Gerald.

"They definitely won't get past Mr Troutman," said Gene. "We need to do a lot more work."

Fleabag was happy enough, though. "These ug-mushrooms make a great ug-pizza topping!" he said.

But a few days later, Gerald, Gene and Fleabag had to put all plans of making perfect vegetables on hold – permanently!

Because when they got home from school that day, something was missing...

"The ug-G-G-Gross-Out ug-D-D-Den!" stuttered Fleabag. "It's ug-vanished!"

"It can't have just gone," said Gene. He began looking around – but then he spotted something even worse than a missing Den...

"Oh no, it's the **Smugleys**!" he cried.

Randy and Mandy Smugley were the twins who lived next door. They loved all things fresh and clean and were the complete opposite of Gerald, Gene and Fleabag.

"Our compost heap has vanished!" said Randy angrily. "Have you stolen it?"

"Only you and your monkey friend would ever think of stealing compost!" said Mandy. "So come on, hand it over!"

"Steal from you?" said Gerald. "You've stolen from us, more like! The Gross-Out Den is missing."

"The Gross-Out Den, missing?" sneered Randy. "I wondered why it smelled slightly less disgusting around here."

"It still smells pretty bad," said Mandy. "Come on, Randy. Let's go and track down *our* compost. And we need to give lovely cuddles to Lamby and Wamby – they've been terribly traumatized by all this."

And with that the Smugleys went off to stroke their pet lambs.

"There's no way the Smugleys would steal our Den," said Gene after they'd gone. "They wouldn't go near it."

"Well, someone ug-has!" said Fleabag.

"But why?" asked Gerald. "And why steal the Smugleys' compost?"

"Something strange is going on here," said Gene.

"Well, we had better ug-find out what ug-soon," said Fleabag, gathering up his possessions, which had been strewn across the garden. "Because I'm ug-homeless!"

5 Meanwhile, on the top floor of the Moldfinger Building, something even more disturbing was happening...

Sir Godfrey Moldfinger, the quiet unassuming mushroom magnate and owner of Moldfinger Mushroom Technologies, was about to undergo a massive makeover.

"I'm sick of just being rich and only owning a mushroom business," the disgruntled tycoon said. "I want more! I want people to take notice of *me*."

"What was that, Sir Godfrey?" said Miss Grubbypenny. "I was busy filing my nails."

"That's EXACTLY what I'm talking about!" boomed Sir Godfrey. "I know you've only just started working here, but do pay attention, Miss Grubbypenny. Now, is everything in place for my makeover?"

"Oh yes, of course," said Miss Grubbypenny.

"Excellent," said Sir Godfrey, walking into his office. "It is time to say goodbye to the old fuddy-duddy Sir Godfrey and hello to Moldfinger, the despotic super-villain!"

"I'm sending the sidekick applicants in, Sir Godfrey,"
Miss Grubbypenny buzzed through the intercom.

"The scary pets have arrived," buzzed Miss Grubbypenny. "Perfect to stroke while hatching an evil plan. Also ideal for unleashing on enemies."

GET THAT THING OUT OF HERE. I'M ALLERGIC TO CA-CA-CATCHOO ... CATS!

OK, IT'S SCARY, BUT I'M GOING TO NEED A HUGE POOPER-SCOOPER...

TOOTHY? TICK! VICIOUS PERSONALITY? TICK! PORTABLE YET INTIMIDATING? DOUBLE TICK!! A GUATEMALAN ATTACK HAMSTER IT IS!!!

"And finally: the tailors," Miss Grubbypenny buzzed again. "They all specialize in outfits for the modern despot about town. They're on their way in..."

HMM. I LIKE THE CHEVRONS, BUT IT'S SAYING "OUT-OF-SHAPE ATHLETE" RATHER THAN "OUT-OF-CONTROL SUPER-VILLAIN".

THE GOTHIC LOOK IS **SOOO** LAST YEAR...

SINISTER? TICK!
POCKET FOR GUATEMALAN-ATTACK-HAMSTER TREATS? TICK!
LOW-MAINTENANCE-NO-NEED-TO-IRON FABRIC? DOUBLE TICK!!
THE DOUBLE-BREASTED DOOM-SUIT IT IS!!!

"Meet the new me, Miss Grubbypenny!" gloated Sir Godfrey. "I've got the look, the vicious pet and the evil assistant. Oddchore, meet Miss Grubbypenny—"

"But, Sir Godfrey," interrupted the burly man, "my name's Cyril Gormley."

"Remember what I said about agreeing with everything I say?!" said Moldfinger in a low menacing voice. "Now, where was I... Oh yes... From now on I will be known simply as **'MOLDFINGER'!! AND I WILL NEVER BE IGNORED AGAIN!!**"

Unaware of the sinister events unfolding at the Moldfinger Building, Gerald, Gene and Fleabag were still trying to find the missing Gross-Out Den. But while Gerald and Gene searched the garden, Fleabag had other ideas.

"Meet the new ug-me," he said, dangling from a wire attached to a tree. "It's ug-time to do what Brock Moleman would ug-do. **Meet ug-Fleabag Monkeyface, Gross-Out Special Agent!**"

Suddenly there was a loud crack – and the branch Fleabag was hanging from snapped. He landed in a heap on the ground, making Gerald and Gene laugh out loud.

But Fleabag just stood up, brushed himself down as though nothing had happened and began speaking in a bold confident voice. "I should think we are looking for a collector. Someone who appreciates the smellier things in life. And who better to hunt down a lover of gross-out than us?"

Gerald and Gene stared at him in amazement.

Fleabag carried on, oblivious. "We're dealing with a heist of spectacular gross-out proportions here. We have no option but to go undercover and solve it ourselves."

"Fleabag?" said Gene cautiously. "Are you all right?"

"All right?" said Fleabag. "I've never felt better!"

Gerald nudged Gene. "What's going on and what happened to the 'ugs'? Fleabag sounds almost ... *intelligent.*"

"I know," agreed Gene. "Maybe *we* should fall out of a tree too."

"The important thing to decide now," said Fleabag, ignoring Gene, "is where I'm going to reside."

"I could dig a hole in the ground, I suppose," he continued in a sad voice. "It wouldn't be much, but at least it would be *my* hole – and secret agents have to be resourceful."

"You can't live in a hole in the ground," said Gerald. "You'll have to move in with me."

"Great!" said Fleabag happily. "I'll be no trouble! Your parents won't even know I'm there!"

7 The trouble was that the new-look Secret Agent Fleabag was nothing but trouble and Gerald's parents definitely *did* notice he was there!

He caused chaos at breakfast by ransacking the kitchen to check for hidden microphones and cameras.

While his hand-to-hand combat practice caused even more trouble...

And bath-time was a complete disaster...

But, at heart, Fleabag was still a creature of habit – and he insisted on having a bed just like his old one in the Gross-Out Den...

"We need to find the Gross-Out Den – and soon," Gerald said the next day. He and Gene were in the garden watching Fleabag build a strange looking device.

"Fleabag, what is *that* thing?" asked Gene.

"It's my very first gadget. I call it the **Compost Detector**," said Fleabag proudly. "No one is going to get away with a gross-out crime with me on the case!"

Meanwhile, Moldfinger was revealing his dastardly plot...

"Mushrooms have made me rich, very rich," purred the despot. "But they have not made me famous. What I want now is fame! And I have found just the way to get it. **Soon everyone will know and fear the great Moldfinger!**"

"What's in the box?" asked Oddchore. "A new super-tasty mushroom to outsell all other varieties?"

"A super-tasty mushroom? Pah!" scoffed the despot, beaming at the strongbox on his desk. "That's why I'm the super-villain and you're the sidekick."

"You can leave us, Miss Grubbypenny," Moldfinger continued. "This is for Oddchore's eyes only."

After Miss Grubbypenny had gone, Moldfinger lifted the lid to reveal a glass case full of ... mushrooms.

"They don't look very tasty," mumbled Oddchore. "In fact, they look disgusting."

"I told you – this is not about taste," barked Moldfinger. "These are the fastest growing mushrooms in the world. If I were to open this glass case, they would expand to fill this room in a couple of minutes. In a couple of hours they would have taken over the entire Moldfinger Building, and in a couple of days—"

"The world?" interrupted Oddchore.

"That was my line!" roared Moldfinger. "Remember who's in charge!"

"But," said Oddchore, "who is going to want a mushroom capable of smothering the world?"

"No one!" said Moldfinger proudly. "That's the point. And unless the World Leaders agree to pay me one million billion zillion dollars in cash, I'm going to unleash these **Super Mushrooms** and destroy the world!"

"Now that *is* odious," said Oddchore.

"Miss Grubbypenny," Moldfinger said into the intercom, "prepare my helicopter. It's time to take a little trip!"

9 Gerald, Gene and Fleabag were still looking for clues when they heard voices coming from next door.

"It's elementary, my dear Mandy," Randy Smugley was saying. He was wearing a strange hat and coat and holding a magnifying glass. "From this piece of fluff, I can tell that the thief was wearing a clown suit and eating a Peach Melba."

Gerald, Gene and Fleabag burst out laughing.

"You've got no chance of cracking the case!" shouted Fleabag. "Leave it to the professionals."

And over the next few days, Gerald, Gene and Fleabag began to make some startling discoveries...

And even when they lost the van's tracks, they were still able to trace the compost, thanks to Fleabag's Compost Detector...

Then, by disguising themselves as road sweeps, they tracked the compost to its final destination...

Armed with this information, they headed back to Gerald's house to discuss their findings.

"Two juices and two biscuits," said Gerald's mum, bringing a tray into Gerald's room. "And a rotten mushroom omelette for Fleabag. I found a bag of Moldfinger mushrooms at the back of the fridge."

"Thank you so very much," said Fleabag, tucking in. "Mouldy mushrooms are my favourite."

"So all the evidence points to Sir Godfrey Moldfinger?" said Gene. "But why would he steal all that compost? And why take the Gross-Out Den?"

"Shh!" said Gerald, pointing out of the bedroom window. "Who's that in the garden?"

"Oh, he's been following us for days," said Fleabag. "Don't worry. I have a plan to catch him. A basic trap."

"A trap?" said Gene, trying not to be annoyed that Fleabag kept coming up with all the ideas. "What kind of a trap?"

"As Brock Moleman says: 'Use the right bait and you'll get the right bite,'" said Fleabag. "I left some mouldy mushrooms under that tree. When he reaches for them, he will trigger a booby trap and be caught in a net. Simple really."

10 **W**hile Gerald, Gene and Fleabag were waiting for the trap to work, a sleek helicopter was flying high above town.

"The only way to truly appreciate the scale of my gloriously devious plot is from the air," said Moldfinger. **"SOON I WILL BE THE MOST POWERFUL MAN ON EARTH!!"**

"How disgustingly evil, sir!" Oddchore chortled. "And no one can stop us!"

"You're getting the hang of this!" said Moldfinger. "Now, below us is the city port..."

Huge cranes were loading enormous crates on to vast cargo ships.

"Pilfered compost from all over the world," said Moldfinger. "Consignments like these have been heading out of the port day and night for weeks..."

"We have cleaned out every farm, industrial greenhouse and municipal park." He cackled. "Every stable, rabbit hutch and garden – there isn't a compost heap or bit of manure left untouched anywhere!"

"But where is it all going?" asked Oddchore, blocking his nose. The smell was unbearable.

"You'll see soon enough," said Moldfinger, steering the helicopter away from the busy port. "So are you enjoying the thrill of flying high above the ground?"

"I'm actually feeling a bit queasy," the sidekick said. "Couldn't we have taken the ferry?"

"*Ferry?* Super-villains like me don't take the *ferry*!" snapped Moldfinger.

An island was emerging on the horizon.

"The first-ever island made entirely from compost. My wondrous **Fungipelago**," said Moldfinger smugly. "Three days ago it was just a dormant volcano sticking out of the sea."

"Are you sure the volcano's dormant?" Oddchore asked nervously.

"Positive," said Moldfinger. "In fact, I'm so confident, I'm using the crater as an extra storage facility. Just wait until you see what's stored in there! Now prepare for landing!"

Back in Gerald's garden, it hadn't taken long for Fleabag's trap to work...

"Who are you?" Fleabag demanded of the man hanging upside down in a large net. "Do you work for Moldfinger?"

"No!" cried the man. "I work for the Government. Now let me go or I'll have you all arrested!"

"The Government?" asked Gene, cutting the man down. "Which department?"

"It's Top Secret. All I can tell you is my name: **Special Agent Double-O-Muck**," said the man, handing Fleabag his identity card. "Come with me to the Ministry and you'll find out everything you need to know."

"Very well," said Fleabag. "But this had better be good."

The special agent escorted them to a waiting limo.

They sped off in the direction of the local dump. "This isn't how I imagined a government building to look," said Gerald, peering out of the window.

"Have you got lost?" asked Fleabag as they drove through the gate and up to the ramshackle building.

As they approached, the front of the building started to judder and shake, before splitting right down the middle to reveal a car park.

"MoG is a top secret organization," said Double-O-Muck, parking among all the blacked-out limos and vans.

"MoG?" said Gene. "What is MoG?"

"I can't tell you, but if you take the lift" – Double-O-Muck pointed to a door in front of the car – "the Commander will meet you. He will explain it all."

**12** Gerald, Gene and Fleabag got into the lift. It seemed to go down for ever.

"Well, it's certainly deep, *deep* undercover," said Gerald.

Eventually, the doors swooshed open to reveal a large shiny high-tech office. People were hurrying about everywhere.

"Welcome to MoG!" said a man in an electric wheelchair. "The name's Moleman, Commander Brock Moleman, and this is the Ministry of Grime."

"*The* Brock Moleman!" gasped Fleabag. "The *real* Brock Moleman. He's my hero!"

"The character in the films is based on me," said Commander Moleman, "but the stories are all made up. I haven't been on an active mission for years. Lost both my knees fighting off a toxic shark. Now, if you'll follow me..."

Commander Moleman led them down a series of corridors to a large room.

"What is the Ministry of Grime?" asked Gene.

"We battle threats to national security that are of a ... how shall we say ... 'grimy' nature," said the Commander. "Our motto is 'Tough on grime, tough on the causes of grime.'"

"So why have we never heard of MoG before?" said Gerald.

"We're a top secret organization," explained the Commander. "And we've been fighting grime for years – but we've never seen anything as menacing as this latest case. Which is why we've brought you in. We've been watching you at work, and you've already been an enormous help."

"Really?" said Fleabag.

"Yes – you led us straight to the culprit: Sir Godfrey Moldfinger," said Commander Moleman.

"Is he using the compost to make more mushrooms?" asked Gene.

"We think it's far more sinister than that," said Commander Moleman, shaking his head. "And that's why we want to recruit *you* as special agents."

"To infiltrate his organization?" said Fleabag.

"Exactly." The Commander smiled. "So do you and your colleagues accept the mission, Fleabag – or should I say – **Special Agent Double-O-Dirt**?"

"Welcome aboard," said the Commander. "I knew you wouldn't let your country down. Now, this is what we have on Moldfinger so far." He pressed a button and a large screen popped up.

"We have discovered that huge quantities of compost are being loaded on to ships and taken out to sea. Moldfinger is using this compost to build an island – his very own Fungipelago!"

"At the base of this island is a volcano – one that could erupt at any moment."

"But first we're going to have to kit you out," continued the Commander.

"You mean gadgets?" said Fleabag excitedly.

"Oh yes." The Commander smiled. "You can't face a super-villain like Moldfinger without gadgets. There's someone you need to meet. Come in, Loo."

A door off the Commander's office swished open and a tall thin man in a lab coat entered.

"This is Loo," said Commander Moleman. "The Ministry of Grime's top gadget boffin."

"Most of the gadgets in the Brock Moleman films are based on Loo's designs," said the Commander as they followed Loo into the testing room.

Loo pointed some of them out:

"Here we have a prototype for the **Melting Dustbin**."

"Watch out – that's **Exploding Toilet Roll**..."

"And this is my pride and joy: the **Flying Garbage Truck**, complete with **Mould-Proof Grabbing Arm**..."

"Of course, none of these are ready yet," said Loo, wiping bits of exploded toilet roll from his jacket. "Now here are *your* gadgets."

They had arrived at a room where everything was already set up for MoG's newest recruits.

"First up – the standard issue watch with abseil cable and the **Special Agent Foldable Jet-Pack**. It's been micro-engineered to fold down to the size of a peanut!"

"**Compost-Proof Wetsuits**... They can withstand even the mouldiest manure!"

"Next – our brand-new **Universal Super-Toxic Melt-Paste**. This stuff is made from thirty-year-old fish scales and will melt everything on contact."

"**Grot Boots** – walk through even the grossest puddle of goo without fear of contamination."

"And, finally, the **Exploding Brussels Sprout**. When detonated it will cover everything in the vicinity in toxic sprout soup."

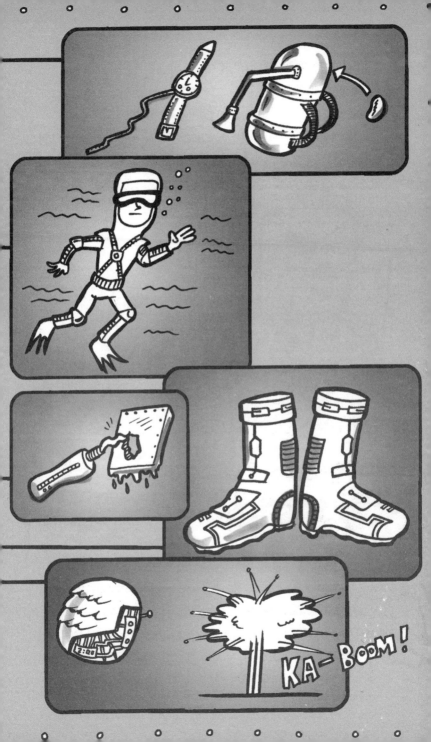

"And one final thing," added the Commander. "Your badges."

Gerald, Gene and Fleabag were now fully fledged special agents!

"Unreal!" said Gene. "So when does our mission start?"

"Start?" said Commander Moleman. "It already has... We need to get to the harbour and fast!"

13 Unaware that MoG's latest recruits were on his trail, Moldfinger was moving into his brand-new lair on the Fungipelago.

"I hope you like the décor," said Miss Grubbypenny. "**Nightmare Lairs International** are the best in the business – they've built evil lairs all over the world!

"Show me around, then," said Moldfinger. "And it had better be **REALLY EVIL**!"

Entertaining room – for schmoozing World Leaders and ensuring they pay the ransom!

Tank containing ferocious Japanese fighting mullet – known for their small jaws but big bite. These fish can nibble through all known substances, and their tank is the perfect way to conceal a control room.

Super-size "Villain" portrait to impress/frighten guests!

Hidden control room, with control panel to unleash doomsday.

Moldfinger, Oddchore and Miss Grubbypenny ended the tour in the **Top Secret Laboratory**.

"What is *that*?" Oddchore pointed to a glass case.

"This is the Gross-Out Den," said Moldfinger. "It's been suspended in preservative – it's where the **Super Mushrooms** came from. One of my drivers noticed some amazing mushrooms at a school. And after a bit of research, we discovered that a couple of children and their monkey friend had made the biggest ever breakthrough in fungal compost technology. So we stole their mushrooms, and once my scientists had made some adjustments of their own, we were ready to go... **And the rest will be history!!!**"

14 Commander Moleman, Gerald, Gene and Fleabag were preparing to board the ministerial submarine.

"We'll be sailing straight to the Fungipelago," said Commander Moleman.

"And what do we do when we get there?" asked Gerald.

"Are we going to fight off henchmen? Have a high-speed boat chase?" said Fleabag.

"No. You're going to a party," said the Commander. "Here's the invitation. The Ministry managed to 'obtain' one..."

To all World Leaders,
Sir Godfrey Moldfinger cordially
DEMANDS *the pleasure of your company at
the house-warming of his brand-new evil lair!*

Not to be missed – there will be a
VERY SPECIAL ANNOUNCEMENT...

"We think he is about to reveal his plan," continued the Commander. "We want you to snoop around. Find out what's happening in that lab. Miss Grubbypenny will report on the announcement."

"But how?" asked Gerald.

"You will pose as heads of state," said the Commander. "You, Fleabag, will be President Porcini. You, Gerald: Minister Morchella, and you, Gene: Chief Ambassador Chanterelle. From the little known Republic of Grossitania."

"I think we may have one small problem," said Gene. "We don't look anything like heads of state going to a party at an evil despot's lair."

"My tailor was meant to meet us here..." said Commander Moleman, looking at his watch.

"It's OK. I've got an idea!" said Gene, secretly pleased to have had an idea before Fleabag. "Follow me!"

Gene knew exactly where to go for the clothes they needed. First, they went to Gerald's second cousin Manuelo, who played in a Mariachi band known for its flamboyant shirts...

WE DON'T WANT ANY FLAMBOYANT PARTY SHIRTS...

BUT IF WE COULD JUST HAVE SOME OF YOURS, COUSIN MANUELO.

Then they went to Gene's next-door neighbour, Professor Bookmus. He was a famous academic who always wore extravagant bow ties.

WE DON'T WANT ANY OLD BOW TIES...

BUT IF WE COULD JUST HAVE SOME OF YOURS, PROFESSOR BOOKMUS.

And, finally, they went to Gerald's great-great-grandfather – the Great Vanishendo. He was a retired stage magician who was known for his trademark velvet suits with lots of secret pockets.

15

Once dressed, Gerald and Gene headed back to the submarine, where Commander Moleman congratulated them on their outfits.

"Great job, gentlemen," he said. "Now, hold on tight – it's time for full throttle!"

After stashing his gadgets in his jacket pockets, Fleabag took up position at the periscope to catch an early glimpse of the Fungipelago.

Now Gerald, Gene and Fleabag had seen many gross things in their lives, but nothing prepared them for the Fungipelago...

They all crowded round the periscope to watch a large island, shrouded in thick smog, loom into view.

"It looks about as welcoming as a squirrel dropping in an ice-cream sundae." Gene shuddered.

"Well, it is made entirely of compost," said Commander Moleman. "On the right is Moldfinger's lair. In the main room there should be a large metal door that leads into the laboratory complex."

What about the boat?" asked Fleabag, adjusting the periscope.

"That's Moldfinger's private yacht. It ferried the World Leaders over from the mainland," said the Commander. "It will return at the end of the party. You need to find out as much as you can and then return on that boat. It will be too dangerous to pick you up in the sub."

"And I'm afraid there'll be no drop-off either," he continued. "Stealth is the name of the game here. You will need to put your special wetsuits on – the waters around here are highly toxic."

"You want us to *swim*?!" gasped Gerald, looking at the murky water.

But Fleabag couldn't have been more excited. "Foul waters hold no fear for Special Agent Double-O-Dirt!" he said, jumping in.

After a short, slimy swim they climbed on to the island, and as you would expect from an island made entirely of compost, it was *not* a pleasant place to be.

"Well, this is like no beach *I've* ever been on," said Gerald, pulling off his mask.

"You would need a gas mask just to make a sandcastle here!" added Gene.

If you're finding this all a bit too disgusting, here's a picture of some really cute caterpillars celebrating Universal-Hug-a-Cabbage Day...

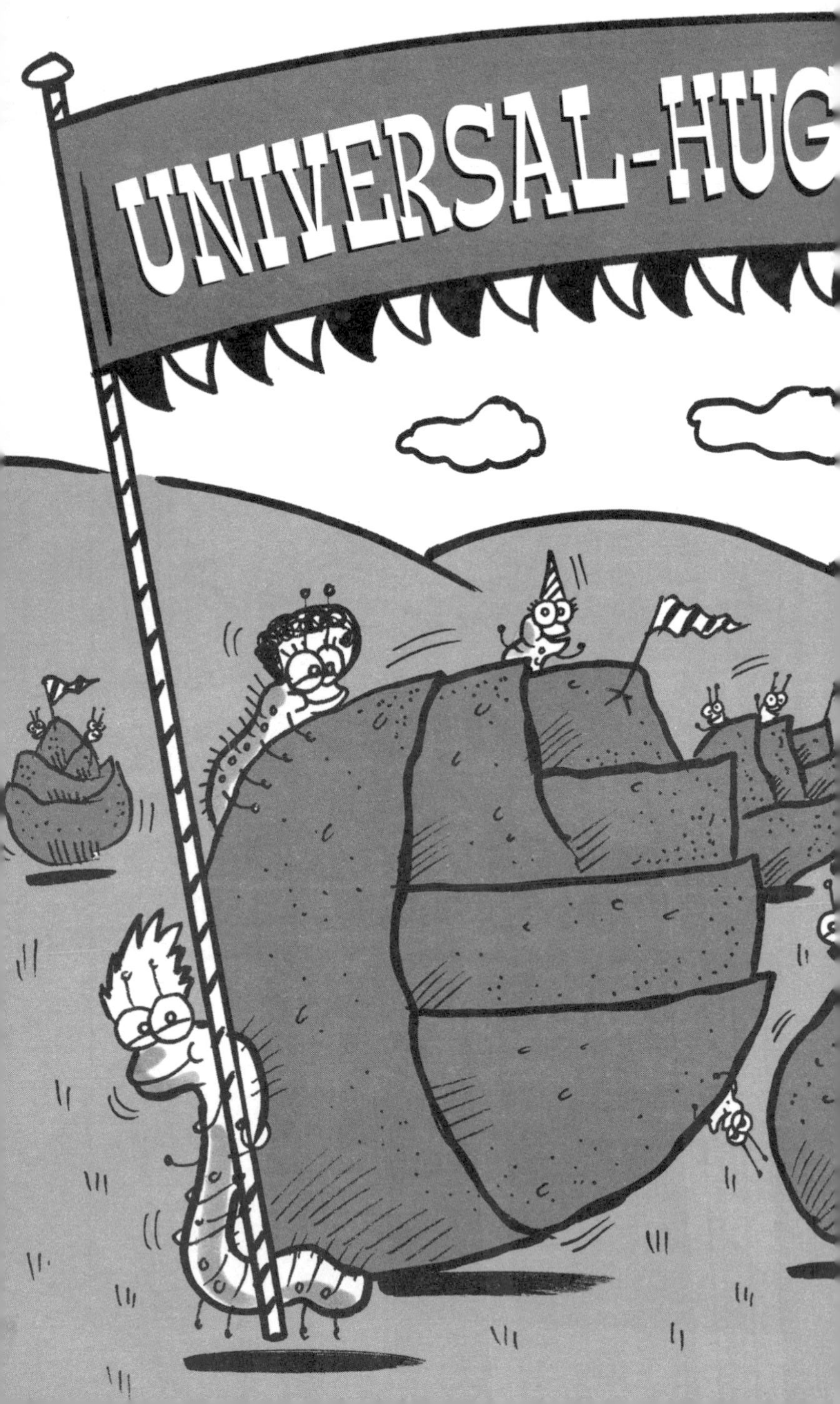
UNIVERSAL-HUG

16 The team headed for Moldfinger's lair.

"Act relaxed, suave and presidential," whispered Fleabag as they unzipped their wetsuits – underneath they were dressed in their snazzy party outfits.

At the entrance to the lair, they were stopped by Moldfinger's security guards...

"President Porcini, Minister Morchella and Chief Ambassador Chanterelle from the Republic of Grossitania," said Fleabag smoothly.

After double checking their invitation, the security guards waved them in...

"Let's get a drink and mingle," suggested Gerald, once they were safely inside.

LONG ISLAND MOULDY MUSHROOM ICED TEA, PLEASE. SHAKEN NOT STIRRED.

Drinks in hand, they tried to blend in ... until they saw something much scarier than any security guard...

OH NO! IT'S THE SMUGLEYS!

"What are you losers doing here?" Randy grimaced.

"Never mind what *we're* doing here, what are *you* doing here?" asked Gerald. "You're not World Leaders!"

"Neither are you! And we were invited," said Mandy. "Daddy plays golf with Sir Godfrey."

"But we wish we hadn't come – have you noticed the smell around here?" said Randy, wrinkling his nose. "We're beginning to think Sir Godfrey might have had something to do with our missing compost. It's time to look for clues, Mandy!"

And with that Randy and Mandy pulled out a pair of magnifying glasses and began scrutinizing every object in the room...

MMM. THIS FLOOR SHOWS CLEAR EVIDENCE OF—

Security was soon smelling a rat ... and a large burly man approached the Smugley twins.

"I'm Oddchore. Moldfinger's Head of Security," he said in an unfriendly voice. "Who are you?"

"Randy and Mandy Smugley – private detectives," said Mandy proudly.

"We know something fishy is going on and we intend to find out what," said Randy.

"If it's *fishy* things you're interested in, then come this way," said Oddchore, bundling the twins through an open door. "We have a private cabin with a lovely sea view – and a nice solid *lockable* door. You can stay there until the boat returns to the mainland."

Just as Oddchore was jostling the Smugleys out of the room, a message boomed out...

LADIES AND GENTLEMEN! MOLDFINGER IS ABOUT TO MAKE HIS SPECIAL ANNOUNCEMENT – AN ANNOUNCEMENT NONE OF YOU CAN AFFORD TO MISS!!!

This was the chance Gerald, Gene and Fleabag had been waiting for! While the World Leaders were listening to the announcement, they could get to work.

17 It didn't take long to identify the door to the laboratory complex.

"It won't budge," said Fleabag, tugging on the door handle. "Time to use the **Universal Super-Toxic Melt-Paste**." He carefully squirted some of the toxic liquid into the keyhole – the lock immediately started to bubble and melt, and after a few seconds, the door popped open.

Through the open door they could see a long corridor. But before they could go inside, they heard a voice in the distance...

"President Porcini, Minister Morchella, Chief Ambassador Chanterelle!" the voice called. "Where are you? You're missing the announcement!"

It was Oddchore!

The three special agents quickly charged through the door and slammed it shut behind them.

"I think he saw us," said Gene.

"We don't have much time then," said Fleabag. "To the Laboratory!"

They snuck down the corridor.

"Look, there's a lift," whispered Gene.

"This is easy," said Gerald as they got in and the doors slid shut behind them.

"Not that easy," said Fleabag, pointing at the lift's control panel. "You need a key to access the **Top Secret Laboratory**. Let's go to the roof instead. I've had an idea."

"I can't believe Fleabag is *still* having all the ideas," Gene hissed to Gerald.

"I know," whispered Gerald. "That was some bump on the head!"

A few minutes later, Gerald, Gene and Fleabag stepped out on to the roof.

"If we can't get through the door, we'll just have to use a window," said Fleabag, explaining his plan. **"It's swing time!"**

"Swing time?" said Gerald. "But we're so high up..."

"You'll just have to hold on tight, then," said Fleabag, pulling the abseil cord from his watch. "Now, all we need is this pole..."

Meanwhile, Moldfinger was addressing the World Leaders...

The World Leaders gasped at Moldfinger's odious plot, but they were not about to give in to his insane demands.

THESE THREATS ARE PREPOSTEROUS!

THIS IS AN OUTRAGE!

WE'LL NEVER PAY!

"You disappoint me," said Moldfinger in a calm voice. "And you leave me no choice. My yacht will return you all to the mainland. Tell your people to prepare for a plague of mushrooms. **NOTHING CAN SAVE YOU NOW!!!**"

19 **W**ith the cord secured around the flagpole at the top of the laboratory tower, Gerald, Gene and Fleabag began to inch down the side of the building.

"Don't look down," Fleabag said as they came level with the Top Secret Laboratory. He tried to open the nearest window, but it was locked, and so were all the others.

"How are we going to get in?" asked Gerald.

"Time for some Gross-Out Power!" said Gene.

Fleabag took a deep breath and unleashed a skyscraper-wobbling **turbo sneeze**! The window buckled, then smashed.

They were now inside Moldfinger's Top Secret Laboratory! And there before them, in a large glass case, was the Gross-Out Den!

"So it *was* him who took it!" said Fleabag. "But why?"

Another even larger glass case stood beside it.

"Your mushrooms!" cried Gerald. "Wow! Look at them now!"

Just then the door of the lab slammed open and Oddchore appeared. "Mr President, you seem to have got rather lost," he said.

"We were looking for the ... er ... bathroom," said Fleabag.

"Of course," said Oddchore. "And you *accidentally* fell through the window..."

"Yes – your lift is most ... confusing," said Gerald. "Now, if you will just show us to the toilet—"

"I've got a better idea," Oddchore interrupted. "Why don't I take you to Moldfinger's private suite instead? I'm sure he would love to meet you and you can use his toilet while you're there."

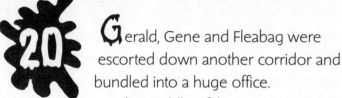

20 Gerald, Gene and Fleabag were escorted down another corridor and bundled into a huge office.

In the middle of the room was a vast desk and behind that, a large chair. It swivelled to reveal ... Sir Godfrey Moldfinger!

"Well, well, His Excellency, the President of Grossitania, and his delegation," he said smugly. "I gather you got 'lost'."

"These three have been acting suspiciously from the start," said Oddchore.

"You see this hamster?" Moldfinger said, stroking his pet. "It's a Guatemalan Attack Hamster. One click of my fingers and it will nibble your knuckles clean off!"

"I should warn you – I bite back!" said Fleabag.

"Ah-ha! I knew it. You are far too brave for a politician. You're working for MoG!" said Moldfinger.

"Ministry of Grime?" said Fleabag. "Never heard of it..."

"The game is up," Moldfinger said. "I know you're a secret agent. I should have known Commander Moleman wouldn't have the guts to come himself. So he got you to do his dirty work. Now, tell me your real name."

"The name's Monkeyface, Fleabag Monkeyface," said Fleabag bravely.

"So, Mr Monkeyface, you saw the Super Mushrooms in my laboratory?" asked Moldfinger. "Not that it matters – the whole world is about to see them!"

"Why?" cried Gene. "What are you planning to do?"

"Unleash them!" roared Moldfinger. "The World Leaders refused to pay the ransom, so in a matter of hours the whole world will be covered in fungi. Nothing will survive!!!!"

"Time for Gross-Out Power, Fleabag!" shouted Gene.

But before Fleabag could even muster up a banana burp, Oddchore had grabbed him from behind.

"Samoan neck choke." The sidekick cackled. "More powerful than an anaconda's grip."

"Get your filthy hands off him!" said Miss Grubbypenny. She lunged at Oddchore. **"Flying-weasel kung-fu kick!"**

"You're fast, but not fast enough!" said Oddchore, blocking the kick. **"Nepalese-viper kick-defence!"**

"Aha, **Filipino elbow lock!**" cried Miss Grubbypenny, grabbing Oddchore's arm. "There's no defence against *this*!"

"You are clearly unaware that I am a black belt in **Burmese nose wrestling**," said Oddchore, finally subduing Miss Grubbypenny.

"I always knew there was something strange about you, Miss Grubbypenny!" said Moldfinger. "So *you're* a special agent too! Lock them up, Oddchore. All of them."

Oddchore handcuffed the secret agents to four chairs. Then Moldfinger pressed a button on his desk. A trapdoor swung open, and Gerald, Gene, Fleabag and Miss Grubbypenny were sent flying down a slide!

At the foot of the chute was a huge catapult. The four agents flew through the air again, and landed with a thud on a cliff at the far side of the island.

"We're in grave danger," said Miss Grubbypenny. "Those Super Mushrooms will be spreading all over the island right now."

"But no mushroom can grow that fast," said Gerald.

"They can if they've been made with **super-toxic compost**," said Fleabag. "And then genetically modified!"

"We need to do something – and fast," said Gene. "Look!"

"Super Mushrooms!" cried Fleabag, his nostril hair standing on end. "Headed our way!"

The fungus groped and probed, forcing the four agents to the very edge of the cliff...

"Grot Boots!" Fleabag said. "They're our only hope!"

The threesome quickly put their high-tech boots on.

"But what about Miss Grubbypenny?" said Gerald, realizing they were a pair short.

"It's OK," Special Agent Double-O-Dirt said. "She can hold on to me and I'll turbo-fart us out of here. If there's one gadget MoG can't supply you with, it's **Gross-Out Power**!"

Fleabag let rip. He and Miss Grubbypenny flew through the fungal fingertips, clearing a path for Gene and Gerald to follow them. They were free!

But little did they realize that back at Moldfinger's lair the situation was escalating scarily out of control!

21 oldfinger and Oddchore had taken up their positions in the lair's control room and were preparing to release the mushrooms.

"Everything is in place, sir," said Oddchore.

"Splendid! Splendid!" exclaimed Moldfinger enthusiastically. "Those World Leaders will rue the day they chose to ignore Moldfinger!"

"Execute lair lockdown, Oddchore," he continued. "Soon the world will be a giant mushroom and only we will be safe!!"

"Are you sure we're ready, sir?" said Oddchore. "There will be no going back."

"Super-villains don't 'go back'," said Moldfinger. "They had their chance and they blew it!"

"Lair lockdown in place," confirmed Oddchore.

"Excellent. Now for the **Tracklayer of Terror**!" said Moldfinger as he pressed a large red button.

High above the control room, the volcano began to shake and shudder as the roof over its crater retracted...

CLANK!

Slowly, the Tracklayer of Terror was hoisted up.
It rumbled down the side of the volcano before
making its way to the edge of the island to start its
fiendish work.

"We have a problem," said Oddchore, peering at a security feed. "The MoG agents have evaded the Super Mushrooms and are headed this way."

"Impossible! No man or woman can escape my killer fungus," said Moldfinger.

"This is no ordinary person," said Oddchore. "This is **Special Agent Double-O-Dirt**!"

"He's even more resourceful than I thought," said Moldfinger, stroking his hamster. "Oddchore, arrange a 'welcoming committee' for him..."

22 "What is going on?" asked Fleabag, staring at the volcano.

"The Tracklayer of Terror," said Miss Grubbypenny ominously. "Moldfinger is planning to use it to build a bridge to the mainland. To spread the dreaded mushrooms worldwide!"

"We need to stop it!" said Fleabag.

"It's controlled from Moldfinger's evil lair. I have a map of the island," said Miss Grubbypenny, reaching into a pocket. "But we need to be careful – this place is full of booby traps."

After a few wrong turns, they finally made it to the lair, but they could see no way in, and no matter which gadgets they tried or which Gross-Out Power Fleabag attempted, the doors simply would not open.

"There's got to be another way in," said Fleabag.

"The volcano!" said Miss Grubbypenny. "The underground monorail leads straight into the lair from inside its crater."

"But how do we get in?" asked Gerald, staring up at the huge mountain looming above them.

"My Gross-Out Powers have been pushed to the limit. Let's use the jet-packs," said Fleabag.

He pressed a button on the side of the device and it sprang into shape.

Gerald, Gene and Miss Grubbypenny held on tight as Fleabag fired up the jet-pack. Within seconds, they were soaring up the side of the volcano...

23 Once inside, it didn't take long to find the monorail. Unaware that Oddchore and Moldfinger were already on to them, the four agents leapt on board.

"Quick!" cried Fleabag.

"This volcano doesn't feel very stable," said Gerald as rocks rained down on them. "I think it's about to blow!"

"Just like Commander Moleman predicted," added Gene.

After a hairy ride through the juddering volcano, they finally pulled up inside the lair.

"We don't have much time," said Miss Grubbypenny. "Moldfinger employed some of the world's finest engineers to make the Tracklayer – it won't take it long to build the bridge."

"We need to get to the control centre," said Fleabag.

"It's underneath the mullet tank," said Miss Grubbypenny.

"But where's the door?" asked Gerald.

"We don't have time to find it!" said Gene, pointing out of the window. "Look!"

The bridge was almost complete!

"Right," said Fleabag, "where's the power supply? If we turn that off, Moldfinger won't be able to control the machine remotely."

"It's here," said Miss Grubbypenny, opening a hidden door.

"A quick blast of **earwax pellets** should put that out of action," said Fleabag, aiming at the switch.

There was a loud…

"That should do it! Well done, Double-O-Dirt," said Miss Grubbypenny. "Now all we have to do is get Moldfinger."

"So how *do* we get into the control room?" said Gerald.

"Simple," said a voice behind them. "You swim! Oddchore, seize them!"

And before any of the agents could move, they were grabbed by Moldfinger's burly flunky.

He bundled them towards a large hook that hung over the mullet pool.

"What are you going to do to us?" asked Gene as Oddchore tied all four of them to the hook.

"Feed you to the Japanese fighting mullet, of course," said Oddchore.

"Release the fish!" demanded Moldfinger.

Oddchore lifted a lever and a snarling shoal of voracious fish rushed from their tank into the pool and began circling hungrily.

NOW LOWER THEM IN!
I WOULD LOVE TO STICK AROUND
AND SEE MY FISH GET THEIR DINNER,
BUT I'M OFF TO THE TRACKLAYER OF
TERROR. THE CONTROL ROOM MAY
BE OUT OF ACTION, BUT I CAN STILL **DRIVE**
MY MACHINE TO THE MAINLAND! **SUCH
A SHAME YOU WON'T BE AROUND TO
SEE A MUSHROOM-INFESTED
NEW WORLD ORDER!!!!**

"My feet are getting wet!" cried Gerald.

"Do something, Fleabag!" said Gene.

"Miss Grubbypenny," instructed Fleabag, "grab the sprout-shaped object in my jacket. Gene, take the exploding sprout and pass it to Gerald... Gerald, place it in my hand... Now, everyone, brace yourself!"

Fleabag detonated the **Exploding Brussels Sprout**. The blast smashed through their chains and threw them all clear of the terrifying fighting mullets.

They were free!

"What's going on?" yelled Oddchore, spinning round just in time to see the hoist swinging in his direction. It struck him in the chest with a loud *thwack*. Then Fleabag pounced on him, wrestling the stricken flunky off balance with a **Sumatran chin throttle**.

Oddchore teetered and tottered, then with a final shove, was sent tumbling into the tank.

"Help my shins are being nibbled!" cried Oddchore.

"Now for Moldfinger!" said Fleabag, running for the exit.

"We need to intercept him before he gets to the mainland!" added Gene.

It didn't take long for the four secret agents to locate Moldfinger. They just had to follow the trail of mushrooms.

"Mr Monkeyface!" gasped Moldfinger. "How did you escape?! You have deprived my mullet of a well-deserved snack!"

"Don't worry," said Fleabag. "They won't go hungry. They're tucking into Oddchore."

"How unpleasant for him!" The super-villain cackled heartlessly. "Well, you may have escaped, but you can't stop me. I will simply run you into the ground!"

"Need a lift?" boomed a familiar voice above them. It was Commander Moleman!

"There are microphones and tracking devices in your special agent badges. Sounded like you were in a spot of bother," he explained. "Loo only just managed to finish the **Flying Garbage Truck** in time... Grab a rope and get on board!"

"That was close," said Fleabag as the four agents climbed into the cockpit.

"We've been following your progress," said Commander Moleman. "Very impressive work."

"Now to finish the job," said Fleabag.

"Time to collect the garbage." Commander Moleman smiled.

25 ommander Moleman flew low over the Tracklayer of Terror.

"Get the truck as close as you can," said Fleabag. "Leave the rest to me."

"Be careful!" said Gerald.

"Hold on tight!" added Miss Grubbypenny as Fleabag jumped on to the Tracklayer of Terror.

Fleabag was now face to face with Moldfinger!

"Get away from me, you filthy ape!" cried Moldfinger. "You and your flying dust-bucket will never defeat me!"

"That's where you're wrong," said Fleabag, reaching into his pocket. "I knew this would come in handy. You didn't get *all* my Super Mushrooms. I kept one on me, just in case."

Fleabag bionic-belched into the air. Then, with all his force, he flung the mouldy mushroom at Moldfinger.

ZOOM!

It landed with a loud **SQUELCH!**

"Get this stuff away from me!" wailed Moldfinger, clawing at the mushroom – but it was stuck fast. "I can't see!" he cried as the Tracklayer of Terror swerved dangerously out of control.

The dastardly vehicle dipped and spun, veering wildly. Then, with a loud splash, it tipped up into the sea. Commander Moleman swooped down and seized Moldfinger using the truck's **Mould-Proof Grabbing Arm**.

"I always knew Moldfinger was a 'rubbish' villain." Fleabag chuckled.

"Now let's get back to the mainland," said the Commander. "That volcano is about to blow! Those deadly mushrooms will be destroyed for ever!"

"But first we need to rescue Oddchore from that mullet tank," said Fleabag. "And there's one last thing to pick up from the Top Secret Laboratory..."

26

Commander Moleman hovered over Gerald's back garden and lowered the Gross-Out Den back into position.

"Well, gentlemen, we couldn't have done it without you. The World Leaders are truly grateful for your amazing work," said the Commander. "Is there anything the agency can do for you?"

Gene suddenly remembered Mr Troutman. "Can you deliver some fresh vegetables to our school?" he said. "And explain why we couldn't grow them ourselves."

"Of course," said the Commander.

"Maybe you and Miss Grubbypenny would like to join us for tea?" said Fleabag.

"We're off on our next mission," said the Commander.

"If we need some help we may give you a call!" said Miss Grubbypenny, and with that they were off.

With the Gross-Out Den back in its rightful place, life could finally get back to normal.

"I can't believe we saved the world and met the *real* Commander Brock Moleman," said Gene.

Just then something moved behind the toilet – one of the Super Mushrooms was still alive! As Fleabag dived to grab it, he hit his head on the ceramic toilet pan.

"Are you all right, Special Agent Double-O-Dirt?" asked Gene.

"Ug-who?" said Fleabag, rubbing his head. "Now, who's for an ug-rotten egg ug-sandwich?"

The knock on the head had returned Fleabag to normal!

But for Gerald, Gene and Fleabag normal is never normal for long... And there was a knock at the door.

"Not the Smugleys!" they all said together.

But it wasn't the Smugleys, it was Gerald's mum.

"I've won a competition!" she said excitedly. "We're going on an all-expenses-paid holiday!"

"A holiday! Ug-great," said Fleabag. "What could possibly go ug-wrong on holiday...?"

To discover what *does* go wrong, you'll have to read the next "Digusting Adventure of Fleabag Monkeyface" – which makes this one seem like a five-star vacation in the world's cleanest resort. **Don't say we didn't warn you!!!**

If you can't wait until the next
Fleabag Monkeyface book, here's
a free comic to keep you going.
(It makes perfect on-the-toilet reading!)

FROM RUSSIA WITH SLUDGE

IN A SIBERIAN DEEP-FREEZE FACTORY, SUPER-VILLAIN MAX BLOWFISH IS TURNING TOXIC WASTE INTO ICEBERGS!

I WILL POSITION THESE AROUND THE WORLD, WHERE THEY WILL MELT AND FILL THE OCEANS WITH POISONOUS SLUDGE!

NOT SO FAST, SLIME FEATURES! USING THIS FLAMETHROWER, HIDDEN IN A FUR HAT, I'LL MELT YOUR ICEBERGS BEFORE THEY'RE LAUNCHED.

MY DREAMS ARE MELTING BEFORE MY EYES!

YOU'RE HEADING STRAIGHT TO THE COOLER - YOU'LL BE ABLE TO CHILL OUT THERE. HAVE AN ICE DAY!

GOLDENFLY

DEEP IN THE DESERT, ZOOLOGIST-GONE-BAD
DR KNOWITALL HAS CONSTRUCTED A VAST GLASS DOME...

I HAVE CAPTURED EVERY FLY IN THE WORLD AND TRAINED THEM TO SWARM...! ONCE RELEASED THEY WILL HERD ALL THE WORLD LEADERS INTO MY GIANT VENUS FLYTRAP - THEN I WILL BE IN CHARGE!

JUST AS WELL LOO PROVIDED ME WITH GIANT FLY-SWATTERS CONCEALED IN THESE CUFFLINKS...

THWACK!

SPLAT!

MY PRECIOUS FLIES!

TIME FOR YOU TO BUZZ OFF!

MUCKRAKER

A SPACE SHUTTLE IS ORBITING EARTH, PILOTED BY EVIL INDUSTRIALIST BARON FRANCOIS KAX. IT IS CARRYING A VAST LOAD OF NOXIOUS MUCK...

TIME TO START OPERATION "REVOLTING RAIN"... BUT WAIT... WHAT'S THAT? WHO CAN SURVIVE IN SPACE ON A HANG-GLIDER?!

BROCK MOLEMAN, SPECIAL AGENT, THAT'S WHO! AND I CAN HOLD MY BREATH FOR OVER THREE HOURS. I'VE ALREADY USED SUPER-EXTENDI GUM TO BLOCK THE CARGO BAY DOORS! YOU THINK YOU'RE A STAR, KAX, BUT THERE'S NO SPACE IN THE WORLD FOR THE LIKES OF YOU!

CONFOUND YOU, MOLEMAN!

FLUSHINO ROYALE

THE JET SET IS CRAMMED INTO AN ELEGANT SALON - BUT THIS IS NO CASINO, THIS IS A **FLUSHINO**! A DEADLY GAME IS ABOUT TO UNFOLD AND EXTREMELY BAD BADDIE RAOUL **ROULETTE** IS PLAYING FOR THE HIGHEST STAKES EVER...

ONE OF THESE IS FITTED WITH MY "REVERSE-O-FLUSH" MECHANISM: IT WILL SUCK ALL THE WATER OUT OF THE WORLD'S TOILETS - AND EVERYONE ON THE PLANET WILL BE LEFT "HIGH AND DRY" WITH UNUSABLE LAVATORIES!

I BET THE WORLD ON A SINGLE FLUSH OF A TOILET, MR MOLEMAN - DO YOU DARE PLAY?

NO DICE, ROULETTE! THIS GIANT PLUNGER CONCEALED IN MY SHOE WILL KEEP YOU BOGGED DOWN FOREVER!

CURSES!